The Lo

written by Pam Holden
illustrated by Samer Hatam

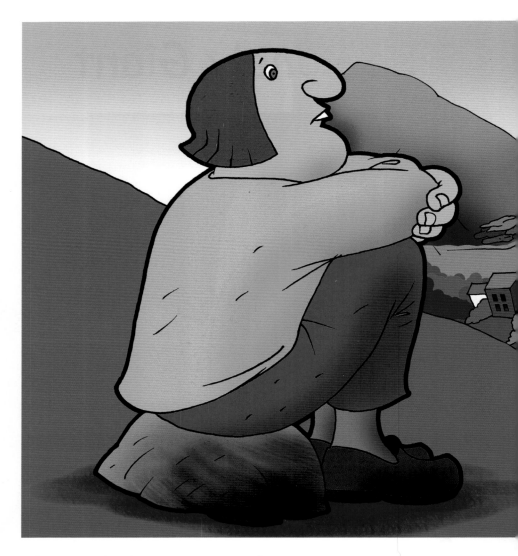

The Lonely Giant was an unhappy, grumpy giant, who lived alone on a high mountain. He was not kind and helpful like the Gentle Giant who lived in the valley below.

"I am tired of living all alone. I wish I had a friend," the Lonely Giant grumbled to himself. "I need someone to talk to and play with, so I will go for a walk to find some friends."

The Lonely Giant came marching down from the
mountaintop to look for a friend. As he walked,
the ground cracked and shook like an earthquake.
Frightened people ran into their houses and shut
the doors tight. All the animals ran quickly to hide,
and the birds squawked as they flapped far away.

4

"I feel so lonely!" roared the giant angrily, stamping his foot. He marched back up his mountain, where he sat all alone, wondering how he could ever find some friends. As he sat there feeling sorry for himself, he noticed some strange and interesting things happening in the valley below...

An enormous tree had fallen across the road, stopping all the traffic. An ambulance could not get past to take a sick person to the hospital. The driver didn't know what to do, but someone kind came to help him. A huge, strong man smiled as he lifted the heavy tree out of the way. He was the Gentle Giant.

"Thank you, Gentle Giant," called the ambulance driver as he quickly drove away to the hospital.

Then the Gentle Giant heard two children calling for
help. Their tiny kitten had climbed onto a high roof,
and it was too frightened to come down. The children
couldn't reach the kitten, and it wouldn't come down
when they called its name. The Gentle Giant reached
up and carefully lifted it down for them.
"Thank you, Gentle Giant," said the happy children.

As the Gentle Giant walked home, he saw a car that was stopped because it had a flat tire. The poor driver couldn't fix it because he didn't have enough tools. The Gentle Giant just lifted the car off the ground while the driver changed the tire. The people got back into the car, smiling at the Gentle Giant as they waved goodbye.

For a long time, the Lonely Giant watched as the Gentle
Giant helped anyone who was in trouble. "He is never
lonely like I am," said the Lonely Giant to himself.
"I must try to be kind and friendly. I could find ways
to help the people and the animals like he does."

Just then, the Lonely Giant heard some loud cries for help. When he saw a sailboat that had been tipped over by a strong wind, he waded into the water to help the sailors. They were very pleased to be rescued, and they waved to him as they sailed away.

Suddenly the Lonely Giant smelled smoke in the air.
Bright orange flames were shooting out of burning
trees in the forest. Frightened birds and animals were
hurrying to get away from the dangerous fire.
The Lonely Giant blew hard on the flames and put out
the fire. As the birds and animals slowly came back to
their homes in the forest, they stopped to say thank
you to him.

The Lonely Giant smiled happily as he walked home.
"I am not alone now. Tomorrow I will be ready to
help any of my new friends who are in trouble,"
he told himself. He knew that he would never be
grumpy or lonely again.